The Kelly Family
Steven, Janet, Marisa and JOHN

Thank you so much for the love and support you have shown me over the years.

The best journeys are measured in friendships not mileage.

This book belongs to:

_____

Harry's Bearded Adventures
Copyright © 2009 by Shawn Geegbae
All rights reserved. No part of this book may be used or reproduced in
any manner whatsoever without written permission.
Library of Congress Cataloging-in-Publication Data
Geegbae, Shawn.

HARRY'S BEARDED ADVENTURES

Shawn Geegbae

Illustrations by Sarita Loredo

Perceval made potions all day and all night.

Red mixed with blue and blue mixed with white, but as the wizard's potion went bubbling away,

His long, grey beard accidentally got in the way!

As night fell, the magic potion grew stronger, while Perceval's grey beard grew longer and longer.

Past the kitchen and through the door, Harry the Beard was attached no more!

Harry walked until he reached
a great green tree.

"May I help?" asked Harry
from beside Santa's sleigh.

"Yes, yes you may," the jolly
man did say.

But the wintry winds and the heavy snow made poor Harry think, "Oh, I'm far too cold."

Buccaneers, pirates, mateys and more were gathered around,

Where treasures of gold can always be found.

"May I help?" asked Harry wishing to sail.

"Yes, yes you may," the one-eyed pirate wailed.

But the sharp swords and salty seas gave poor Harry a fright and he started to wheeze!

Where bunkhouses, tents, and porridge abound, strong men chop big trees down.

"May I help?" asked Harry wanting to build.

"Yes, yes you may," the lumberjack happily trilled.

But the water and sweat made poor Harry think, "Ewww, gross! I'm as wet as a sink."

White, red, blue and orange flowers appear, under a sky that's blue and clear.

May I help?" asked Harry on his merry way.

"Yes, yes you may," the Billy goat bah-h-a-a-d away.

But being dragged made poor
Harry feel these lumps and
bumps may take some time to
heal.

Pieces of gold, patches of clothes, flowers that grow were all over Harry even a red bow.

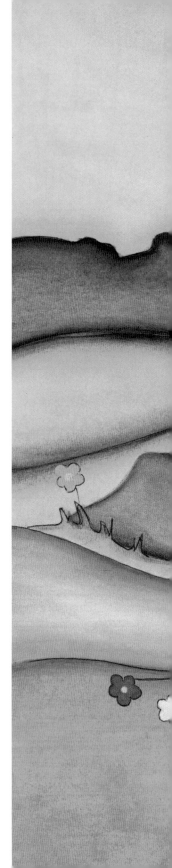

"I must get back on Perceval's chin," Harry said aloud with a slight grin.

So he walked back for years, weeks, and days thinking of all the friends he had made.

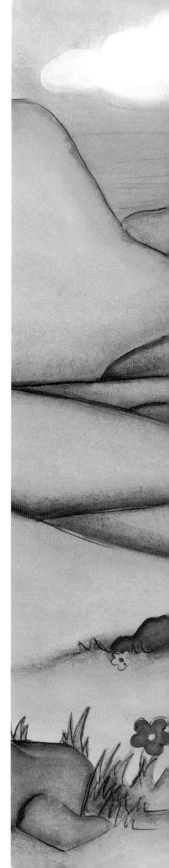

Harry was very happy being
back where he truly belonged,
But the next morning, Perceval
thought, "Where have I gone?"

Shawn Geegbae is an American author and writer. Shawn enjoys entertaining and uplifting his audience through his writing. In addition to writing children's books, Shawn desires to broaden his palate to screenplays and live theater. Shawn is an alumnus of Syracuse University in New York.

Sarita Loredo was born in Reston, Virginia and grew up in the small town of Leesburg. She graduated with a B.F.A from George Mason University's School of Art. Sarita also enjoys photography, painting, drawing, sculpture and textiles.

Made in the USA
Charleston, SC
16 March 2014